Getting to Know Ruben Plotnick

Written by Roz Rosenbluth

Illustrated by Maurie J. Manning

Flash Light PRESS

New York

First Edition - September 2005

Library of Congress Control Number: 2005920616

ISBN 0-972-92255-5

Editor: Shari Dash Greenspan
Graphic Design: The Virtual Paintbrush
This book was typeset in Humana Serif.
Illustrations were rendered using digital pencil, watercolor and chalk.

Distributed by Independent Publishers Group

Flashlight Press • 3709 13th Avenue • Brooklyn, NY 11218
www.FlashlightPress.com

For Sarah, always with me -RR

For my Mummu Irma and Grammy Tillie -MJM

Ruben Plotnick is the coolest kid in my class, and he's known throughout school as "The Plotnick." Everything Ruben does is zany. He smears peanut butter mustaches under his nose at lunch. He blows bubbles with a straw in his chocolate milk. He sits on the windowsill in class and balances books on his head while he reads. He answers questions in a kooky voice, but he always knows the right answers. He's very smart.

Everyone wants to be his friend.

And suddenly one day, for the first time, The Plotnick wanted to come to my house to do homework with me.

I was really glad Ruben wanted to come over, but I was also pretty worried about what he would think of Grandma Rosie. You never can tell what she'll do.

You see, my Grandma Rosie forgets things and mixes things up. Sometimes she sits totally still and won't answer when you talk to her. Other times she rocks so much you'd think she was in some kind of rocking contest.

Her hair is white and she's very pretty. She's a great singer too. Her voice is kind of whispery now, but she knows the words to tons of old songs. She still makes the best chocolate cookies I ever tasted, but sometimes she calls me "little boy" instead of David.

Grandma Rosie is also awesome at checkers, and when she's in the mood,
we have some good, fast games. Of course, in the middle of a move,
she could knock over the board and start an argument with my Grandpa Nate,
who died five years ago. She does this once in a while, and let me tell you,
I jump ten feet every time it happens.

But the weirdest thing is when she's just sitting quietly
humming or drinking tea, and suddenly calls out,
"Nate, let's waltz!"

Since dancing is her favorite thing, whoever's in the room
helps her out of her chair, puts an arm around her waist
and waltzes. Even Martha, our pet schnauzer, gets up
on her hind legs and follows us around.

It's a crazy scene, but it makes Grandma happy.

I love my Grandma Rosie, but I was sure hoping she'd be taking a long nap when I came home with Ruben Plotnick that day.

Naturally Grandma wasn't napping. She was sitting in the kitchen, sipping tea.

"Hi Grandma," I said, hoping she wouldn't call me "little boy." "This is Ruben Plotnick."

Grandma went on sipping.

"Ruben," I said, "this is my Grandma Rosie."

Ruben waved his pinky at her. "Got any chocolate milk?" he asked me.

We didn't have any, so I gave him plain milk, some of Grandma's chocolate cookies, and a straw. Right away he crumbled the cookies into his glass.

"Chocolate milk!" he said, laughing hysterically. He laughs hysterically a lot.

Then he plopped himself into the kitchen sink with his legs dangling over the edge and started blowing bubbles in his homemade chocolate milk.

When Grandma heard the bubble blowing, she looked up at Ruben sitting in the sink. "Hello, little boy," she said in her whispery voice.

Ruben looked at Grandma. I could just imagine him answering questions in class the next day in Grandma's voice. In fact, I expected him to say hello back to Grandma in a funny whisper.

But Ruben only smiled, said hello in his own voice, and went on blowing bubbles. I wished he'd hurry up and finish so we could go to my room, but he was stuck in that sink like he was planted.

Suddenly Grandma Rosie scraped her chair along the floor and tried to get up.

"You want to go to your room, Grandma?" I asked hopefully.

She shook off my hand. "Nate, let's waltz," she said clearly, looking straight at Ruben.

Disaster!

I stepped in front of her and put my arm around her waist.
"Okay, let's waltz," I said. I could just imagine what a ball Ruben would
have with this scene the next day. I could see him acting out the whole thing
in front of the class. All I wanted was to get the dancing over with,
but Grandma wouldn't budge.

"Nate," she said very loudly, still looking at Ruben, "let's waltz!"

And then it happened.

Ruben The Plotnick put down his glass,
wiped his hands on his jeans,
lifted himself out of the sink
and stepped between us.

"She wants to dance with me, not you,"
he said quietly, putting his arm around
Grandma's waist.

And there they were – Grandma and Ruben Plotnick – waltzing around our kitchen, and he was dead serious about it. Not that what he was doing was exactly a waltz. But it was a good enough imitation, and Grandma sure looked happy.

I thought I knew "The Plotnick," but boy, was I wrong.
Ruben, the class clown, had this perfect situation handed to him,
sure to get a laugh, but he never acted it out, never imitated Grandma's
voice or her dancing. Now I'm happy Ruben met Grandma Rosie.
I learned things about him I never would have guessed from school.

I'm glad I'm really getting to know Ruben Plotnick.

Last night Grandma Rosie looked up from her dinner plate and called out, "I want the little boy in the sink."

Mom sighed and patted Grandma's hand and Dad shook his head sadly, but I knew exactly what she wanted.

She wanted Ruben The Plotnick to put down his glass,
         wipe his hands on his jeans,
                  lift himself out of the sink,
                           put his arm around her waist…

...and waltz!

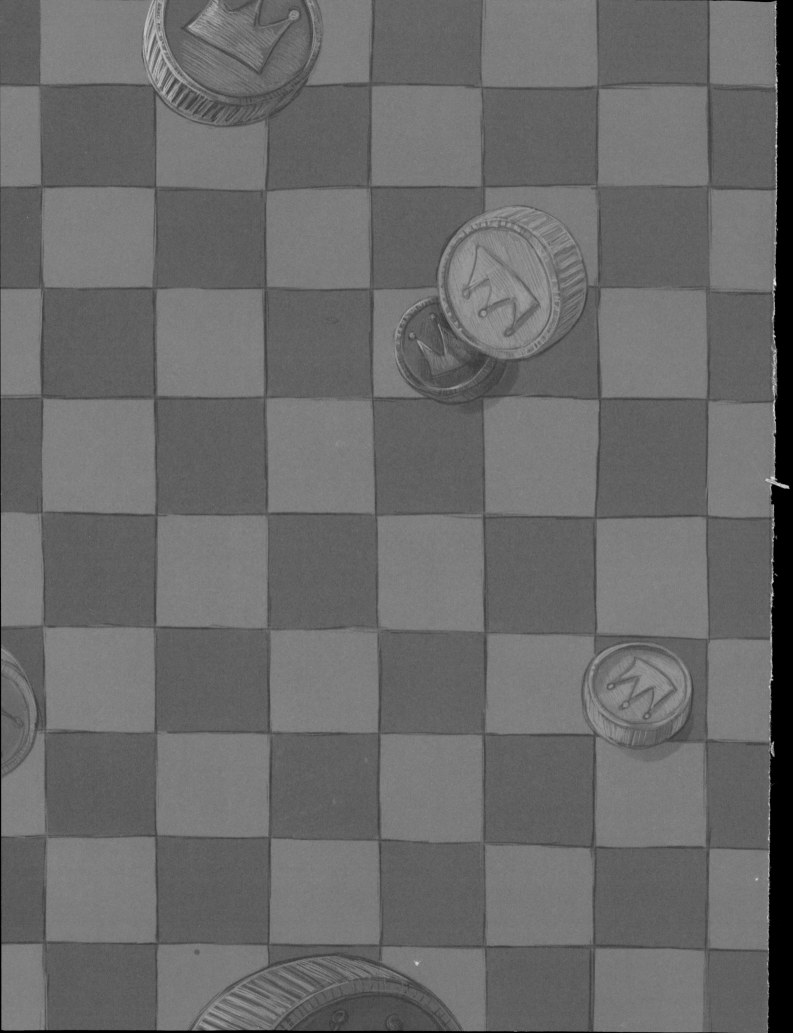